THIS WALKER BOOK BELONGS TO:

_____

_____

_____

_____

For Rory
& Conor

First published 1997 by Walker Books Ltd, 87 Vauxhall Walk, London SE11 5HJ

This edition published 1999

2 4 6 8 10 9 7 5 3 1

© 1997 Penny Dale

This book has been typeset in Garamond ITC Book.

Printed in Hong Kong/China

British Library Cataloguing in Publication Data
A catalogue record for this book is available from the British Library.

ISBN 0-7445-6953-2

Big Brother, Little Brother

Penny Dale

WALKER BOOKS
AND SUBSIDIARIES
LONDON • BOSTON • SYDNEY

When Little Brother cries like this,
who knows why?

Big Brother.

"He wants to eat the same food as me.

See, I knew, didn't I?"

When Little Brother looks like this,
who knows why?

Big Brother.

"He wanted you to take the dog away.
He's scared.

See, I knew, didn't I?"

When Little Brother shouts like this,
who knows why?

Big Brother.

"He wants to be in here with me.

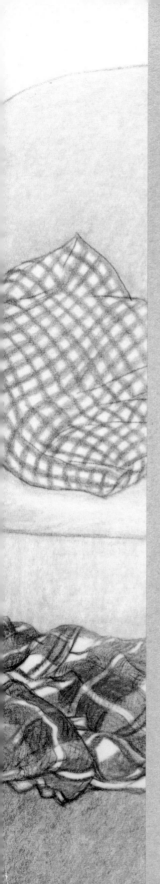

See, I knew, didn't I?"

But when
Little Brother
wants
Big Brother's
truck …

what
does
Big Brother
say?

"No!
You can't
have it.
It's mine."

When Big Brother puts his truck away,

and Little Brother takes it,

and Big Brother can't find it,

Big Brother starts to cry.

When Big Brother cries like this,
who knows why?

Little Brother.

"You knew.
You brought me back my truck.

We're brothers, that's why."

MORE WALKER PAPERBACKS
For You to Enjoy

Also by Penny Dale

TEN IN THE BED

"A subtle variation on the traditional nursery song, illustrated with wonderfully warm pictures …
crammed with amusing details." *Practical Parenting*

0-7445-1340-5   £4.99

TEN OUT OF BED

"A counting backwards version of 'Ten in the Bed'… Penny Dale's warm and
distinctive illustrations are full of action and movement … lots to look at,
smile at and talk about." *Children's Books of the Year*

0-7445-4383-5   £4.99

WAKE UP, MR. B!

Commended for the Kate Greenaway Medal, this is the simple account of a small girl
playing some imaginative early morning games with her dog.

"Perceptive, domestic illustrations fill a varied cartoon-strip format …
making this a lovely tell-it-yourself picture book." *The Good Book Guide*

0-7445-1467-3   £4.99

Walker Paperbacks are available from most booksellers, or by post from B.B.C.S., P.O. Box 941, Hull, North Humberside HU1 3YQ

24 hour telephone credit card line 01482 224626

To order, send: Title, author, ISBN number and price for each book ordered, your full name and address, cheque or
postal order payable to BBCS for the total amount and allow the following for postage and packing:
UK and BFPO: £1.00 for the first book, and 50p for each additional book to a maximum of £3.50.
Overseas and Eire: £2.00 for the first book, £1.00 for the second and 50p for each additional book.

Prices and availability are subject to change without notice.